A Note to Parents and Caregivers:

Read-it! Readers are for children who are just starting on the amazing road to reading. These beautiful books support both the acquisition of reading skills and the love of books.

The RED LEVEL presents familiar topics using common words and repeating sentence patterns.

The BLUE LEVEL presents new ideas using a larger vocabulary and varied sentence structure.

The YELLOW LEVEL presents more challenging ideas, a broad vocabulary, and wide variety in sentence structure.

The GREEN LEVEL presents more complex ideas, an extended vocabulary range, and expanded language structures.

When sharing a book with your child, read in short stretches, pausing often to talk about the pictures. Have your child turn the pages and point to the pictures and familiar words. And be sure to reread favorite stories or parts of stories.

There is no right or wrong way to share books with children. Find time to read with your child, and pass on the legacy of literacy.

Adria F. Klein, Ph.D.
Professor Emeritus
California State University
San Bernardino, California

Managing Editors: Bob Temple, Catherine Neitge
Creative Director: Terri Foley
Editor: Jerry Ruff
Editorial Adviser: Mary Lindeen
Designer: Melissa Kes
Page production: Picture Window Books
The illustrations in this book were rendered digitally.

Picture Window Books
5115 Excelsior Boulevard
Suite 232
Minneapolis, MN 55416
877-845-8392
www.picturewindowbooks.com

Printed in the United States of America.

Library of Congress Cataloging-in-Publication Data
Blair, Eric.
The wolf and the seven little kids: a retelling of the Grimms' fairy tale / by Eric Blair;
illustrated by Brett Petrusek.
p. cm. — (Read-it! readers fairy tales)
Summary: Mother Goat rescues six of her kids after they are swallowed by a
wicked wolf.
ISBN 1-4048-0594-X (reinforced library binding: alk. paper)
[1. Fairy tales. 2. Folklore-Germany.] I. Petrusek, Brett, ill. II. Grimm, Jacob, 1785-
1863. III. Grimm, Wilhelm, 1786-1859. IV. Wolf und die sieben jungen Geisslein.
English. V. Title. VI. Series.
PZ8.B5688Wo 2004
398.2'0943'04529648—dc22   2003028230

The Wolf
and the
Seven Little Kids

By Eric Blair

Illustrated by Brett Petrusek

Special thanks to our advisers for their expertise:

Adria F. Klein, Ph.D.
Professor Emeritus, California State University
San Bernardino, California

Kathleen Baxter, M.A.
Former Coordinator of Children's Services
Anoka County (Minnesota) Library

Susan Kesselring, M.A.
Literacy Educator
Rosemount-Apple Valley-Eagan (Minnesota) School District

PICTURE WINDOW BOOKS
Minneapolis, Minnesota

Once upon a time, there was a mother goat who had seven kids. She loved them as only a mother could.

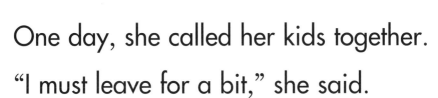

One day, she called her kids together.
"I must leave for a bit," she said.
"Beware of the wolf. You will know
him by his gruff voice and
gray paws."

The kids promised they would be careful. The mother goat went to find food, and the kids locked the door behind her.

Soon, there was a knock at the door. "Open up," said a gruff voice. "Your mother has returned with gifts for you."

"You are not our mother," said one
kid. "She has a soft, sweet voice.
Your voice is rough and raw. You
are the wolf!"

The wolf went away. He bought a box of chalk and ate it. The chalk coated his throat and made his voice sound soft and sweet. Then he went back to the house.

The wolf knocked on the door. "Open up, dear children," he said softly. "I am your mother, and I have something nice for each of you."

But the kids saw the wolf's gray paw against the window. "You are not our mother," one kid said. "She doesn't have gray paws. You are the wolf!" Again, the wolf went away.

Next, the wolf went to the bakery.
"I hurt my paw," he said to the baker.
"Wrap some dough around it." The
baker did as he was told.

Then the wolf ran to the miller.
"Sprinkle some white flour on my
paw," he said. The miller was afraid
of the wolf, so
he obeyed.

The wolf went back to the house. "Open up," he said. "Your mother is back." "It sounds like you, Mother," said one kid.

"But to be sure, show us your paw."
The wolf put his paw on the window.
It was white, so the kids opened the
door. In jumped the wolf!

The kids hid. One slid under the table, and another crawled into the bed. The youngest sat quietly in the clock case.

The wolf found all the kids except the youngest. He ate them in great big gulps. Then the wolf went into a meadow and fell asleep under a tree.

When the mother goat came home, the door was wide open. Tables, chairs, and benches were overturned. She called for her kids, but they were nowhere to be found.

Then the mother goat got near the clock case. Her youngest kid called out. The mother goat helped him to his feet, and he told her what had happened. She cried and cried.

After she had cried for a long time, the mother goat and her youngest kid went outside. They found the spot where the wolf lay sleeping under a tree.

The mother goat saw something moving in the wolf's stomach. *Is it possible that the children are still alive?* she wondered. She told her youngest kid to get scissors, a needle, and thread.

When the kid returned, the mother goat cut open the wolf's stomach with the scissors. As soon as the mother opened the wolf's stomach, all six kids jumped out.

Since the greedy wolf had swallowed them whole, they were alive! The mother goat hugged them.

"Find six stones," the mother goat told her kids. "We will fill the wolf's stomach with them while he sleeps."

The kids gathered the stones and put them in the wolf's stomach. The mother goat sewed up the wolf with the needle and thread.

When the wolf woke up, he went to get a drink at the well. The stones knocked against one another and rattled in his stomach as he walked.

The wolf cried, "Why this rumble and tumble? Why this rattle like bones? I thought I ate six little kids, but it feels more like stones."

When the wolf got to the well, he stooped over to take a drink. The stones made him lose his balance.

The wolf fell into the water. The stones dragged him to the bottom of the well, and he drowned.

When the kids saw this, they cried, "The wolf is dead, the wicked wolf is dead!"

The seven little kids danced with their mother in a circle of joy.

Levels for *Read-it!* Readers

Read-it! Readers help children practice early reading
skills with brightly illustrated stories.

Red Level: Familiar topics with frequently used words and
repeating patterns.

Blue Level: New ideas with a larger vocabulary and a variety
of language structures.

Little Red Riding Hood by Maggie Moore
The Three Little Pigs by Maggie Moore

Yellow Level: Challenging ideas with an expanded vocabulary
and a wide variety of sentences.

Cinderella by Barrie Wade
Goldilocks and the Three Bears by Barrie Wade
Jack and the Beanstalk by Maggie Moore
The Three Billy Goats Gruff by Barrie Wade

Green Level: More complex ideas with an extended vocabulary
range and expanded language structures.

The Brave Little Tailor by Eric Blair
The Bremen Town Musicians by Eric Blair
The Emperor's New Clothes by Susan Blackaby
The Fisherman and His Wife by Eric Blair
The Frog Prince by Eric Blair
Hansel and Gretel by Eric Blair
The Little Mermaid by Susan Blackaby
The Princess and the Pea by Susan Blackaby
Puss in Boots by Eric Blair
Rumpelstiltskin by Eric Blair
The Shoemaker and His Elves by Eric Blair
Snow White by Eric Blair
Sleeping Beauty by Eric Blair
The Steadfast Tin Soldier by Susan Blackaby
Thumbelina by Susan Blackaby
Tom Thumb by Eric Blair
The Ugly Duckling by Susan Blackaby
The Wolf and the Seven Little Kids by Eric Blair

A complete list of *Read-it!* Readers is available on our Web site:
www.picturewindowbooks.com